Miranda's maracas

Lesley Sims

Illustrated by David Semple

Miranda is humming.
She sets up her stall.

She sells big maracas.

They're great fun for all!

The market is bustling.
It's carnival time.

"Hi! Try my maracas!" she writes on a sign.

HI! TRY MY MARACAS!

But no one comes over,
to try or to buy.

Miranda packs up and
heads home with a sigh.

Next door, little Rattlesnake's
started to cry.

His mother is frowning.

He won't stop this noise.

"He's too sad to play.
He's ignoring his toys."

"He wails and he wails.
It's all such a battle."

"I know what will help you,
so just dry your eyes!"

She trots to her workshop
and makes a surprise.

The next day, she plods to her stall.
She feels blue.

A crowd is around it.
There's quite a to-do.

Miranda is baffled.
Is there a mistake?

She sees little Rattlesnake.

Shake-a-shake-shake!

Now everyone's buying.

They're nearly all gone!

About phonics

Phonics is a method of teaching reading which is used extensively in today's schools. At its heart is an emphasis on identifying the *sounds* of letters, or combinations of letters, that are then put together to make words. These sounds are known as phonemes.

Starting to read

Learning to read is an important milestone for any child. The process can begin well before children start to learn letters and put them together to read words. The sooner children can discover books and enjoy stories and language, the better they will be prepared for reading themselves, first with the help of an adult and then independently.

You can find out more about phonics on the Usborne Very First Reading website, **veryfirstreading.com**. Click on the **Parents** tab at the top of the page, then scroll down and click on **About synthetic phonics.**

Phonemic awareness

An important early stage in pre-reading and early reading is developing phonemic awareness: that is, listening out for the sounds within words. Rhymes, rhyming stories and alliteration are excellent ways of encouraging phonemic awareness.

In this story, your child will soon identify the *m* sound, as in **Miranda** and **maraca.** Look out, too, for rhymes such as **snake – shake** and **noise – toys**.

Hearing your child read

If your child is reading a story to you, don't rush to correct mistakes, but be ready to prompt or guide if he or she is struggling. Above all, do give plenty of praise and encouragement.

Edited by Jenny Tyler
Designed by Sam Whibley and Hope Reynolds

Reading consultants: Alison Kelly and Anne Washtell

First published in 2021 by Usborne Publishing Ltd., Usborne House, 83-85 Saffron Hill,
London EC1N 8RT, England. usborne.com Copyright © 2021 Usborne Publishing Ltd.